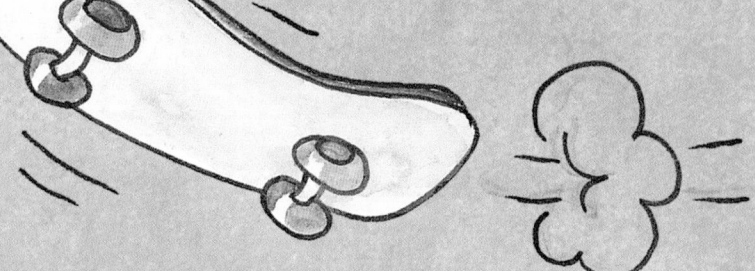

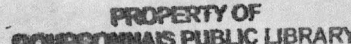

For Emma, George and Oscar — S.S.

For Ella, Dan and all my family — A.S.

For Jessie, Lola and Lenny — R.A.

JANETTA OTTER-BARRY BOOKS

The authors, illustrator and publishers would like to thank Aminder and Tatinder Virdee
and all the children, families and professionals who contributed ideas and inspiration for this book.

Max the Champion copyright © Frances Lincoln Limited 2013
Text copyright © Sean Stockdale and Alexandra Strick 2013
Illustrations copyright © Ros Asquith 2013
The right of Alexandra Strick, Sean Stockdale and Ros Asquith to be identified as the authors
and illustrator of this work has been asserted by them in accordance with the Copyright,
Designs and Patents Act, 1988 (United Kingdom).

First published in Great Britain in 2013 and in the USA in 2014 by
Frances Lincoln Children's Books,
74-77 White Lion Street, London N1 9PF
www.franceslincoln.com

A catalogue record for this book is available from the British Library.

ISBN 978-1-84780-388-7

Illustrated with watercolour

Set in Cronos

Printed in Dongguan, Guangdong, China by Toppan Leefung in March, 2013.

135798642

MAX THE CHAMPION

Written by **Sean Stockdale and Alexandra Strick**

Illustrated by **Ros Asquith**

F

FRANCES LINCOLN
CHILDREN'S BOOKS

Max loved sport.
Night and day,
it filled his dreams!

At the breakfast table,
Max
dived
into his cereal.

RING!

Then he buckled his helmet
and **sped** off to school.

He **never** missed a turn.

At school, Max and his friends **flew**
through their handwriting practice.

SPLISH SPLOSH

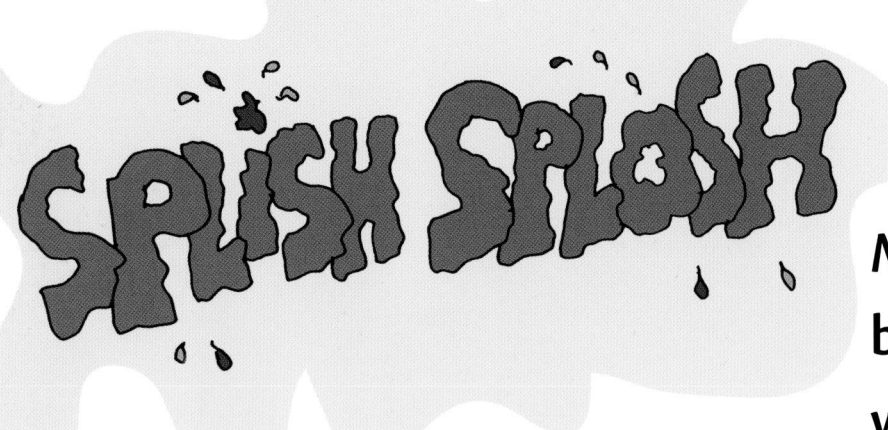

Max gave art his best shot, but somehow his picture was a bit **different**.

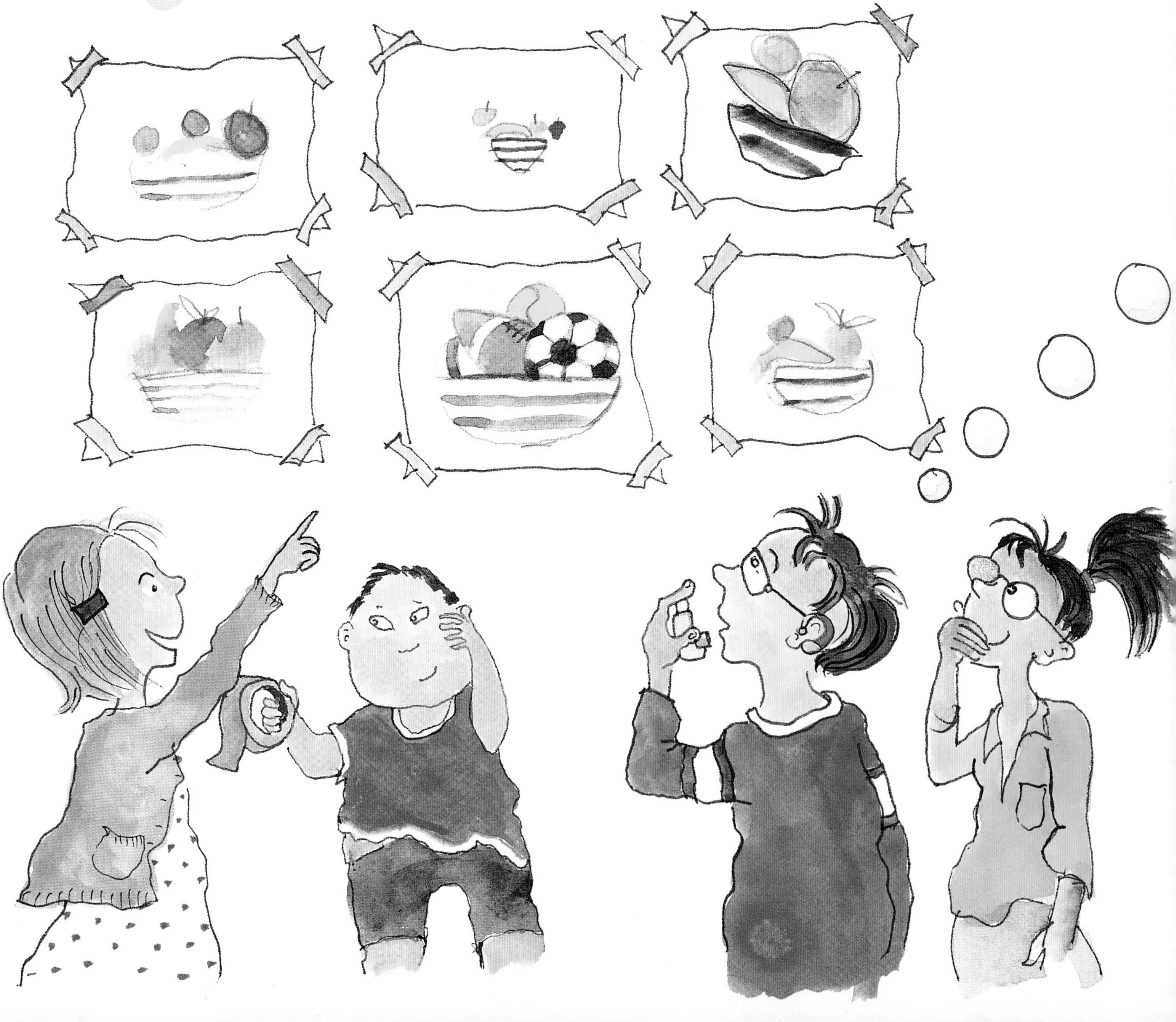

That afternoon, Max's school had **a fun** sports tournament with another school.

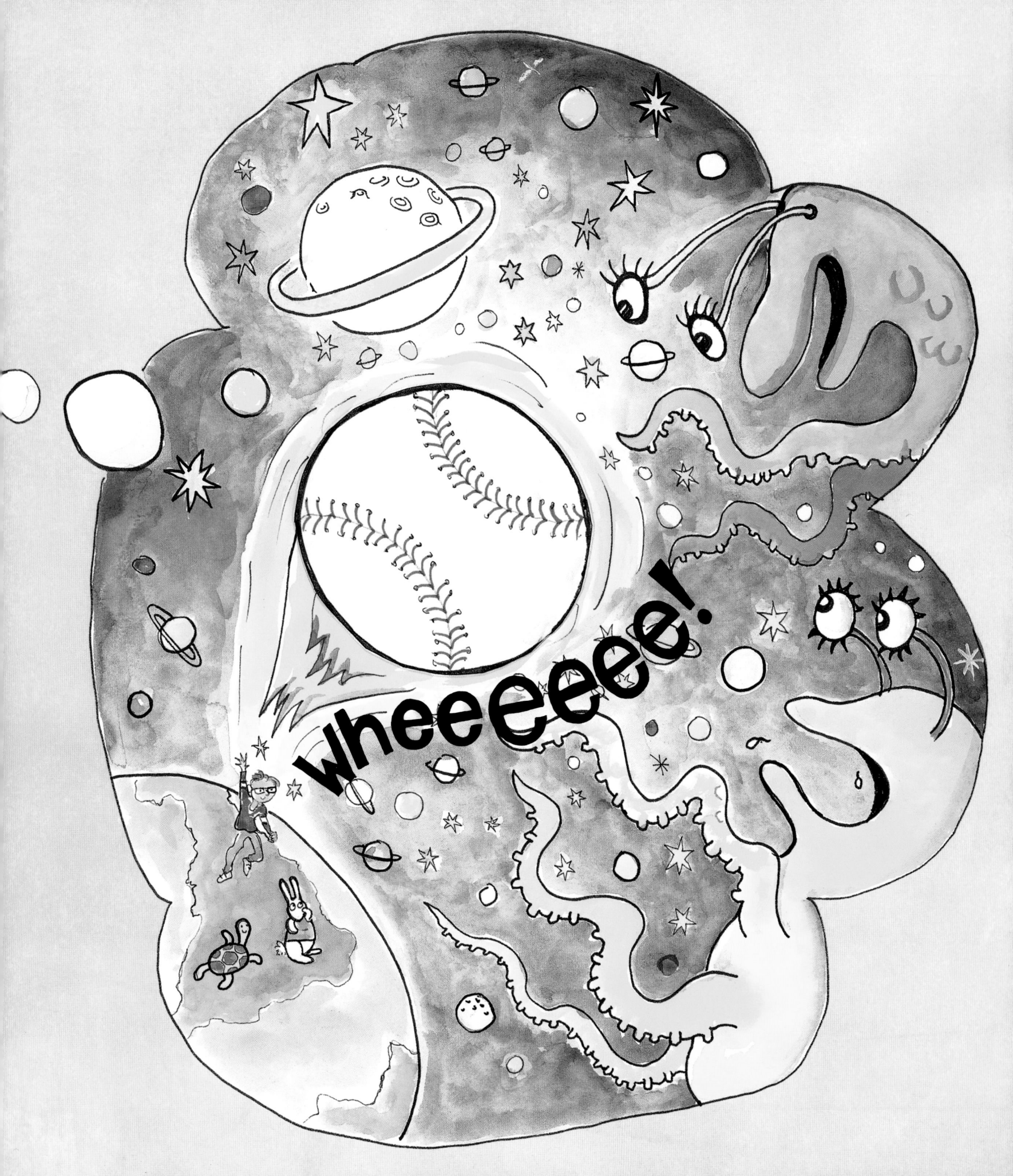

To celebrate winning the tournament, there was a special assembly at school. Everyone **cheered** as Max and his friends received their trophies.

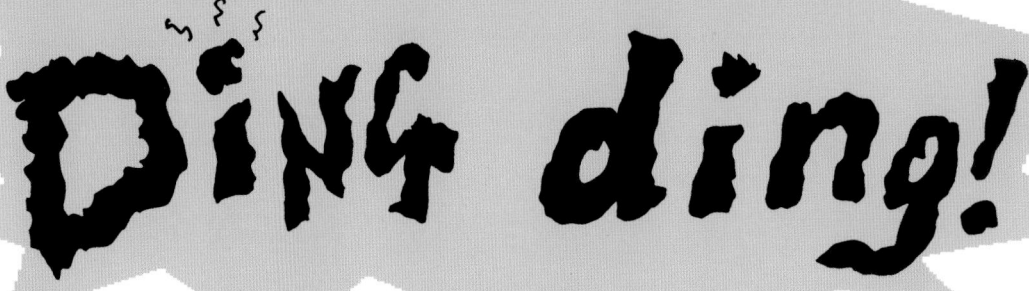

DING ding!

The school bell rang
and it was time to go home.
Max **shot** out of the door...

and cycled home with his friends.

ZOOM!

That night, as Max snuggled into bed,
a smile crept across his face.
Then he drifted happily off to sleep.
What a **dream** of a day.

No prizes for guessing
what he dreamed about!

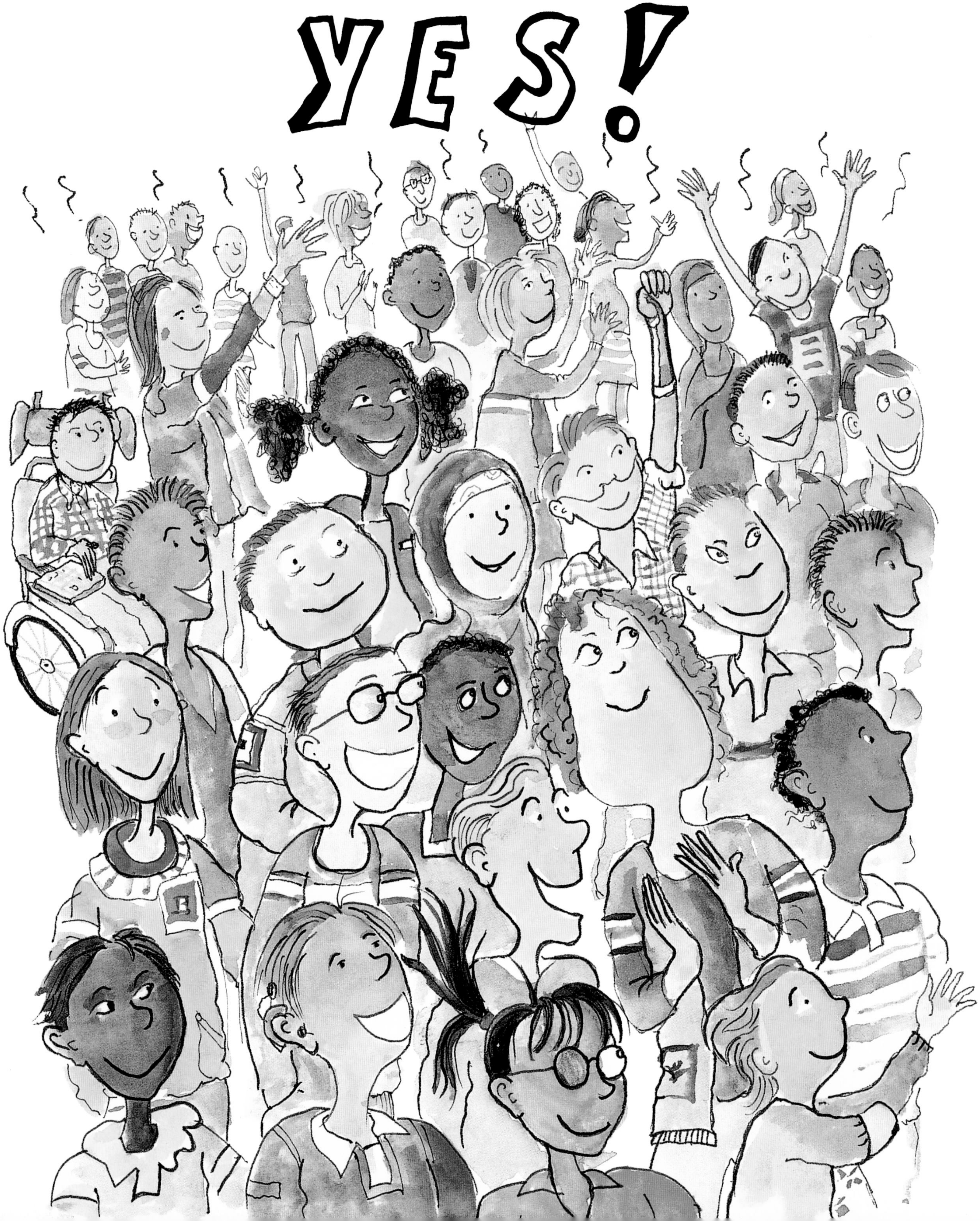
YES!

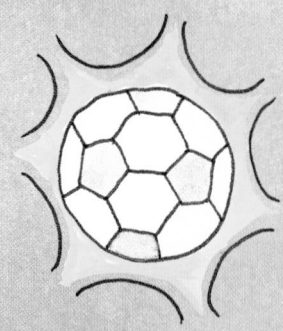

Max, Booktrust and nasen

Sean and Alexandra's idea for *Max the Champion* came about through their work with Booktrust and nasen.

Booktrust is the national charity which aims to inspire everyone to enjoy books and reading. Nasen is the leading UK professional association embracing all special and additional educational needs and disabilities. Booktrust and nasen believe that we need stories and pictures which reflect all children – including children with additional needs.

Max is first and foremost a fun picture book about a boy with a powerful imagination. It also shows us that deaf and disabled children can – and should – be included, both in stories and in life.

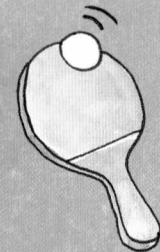

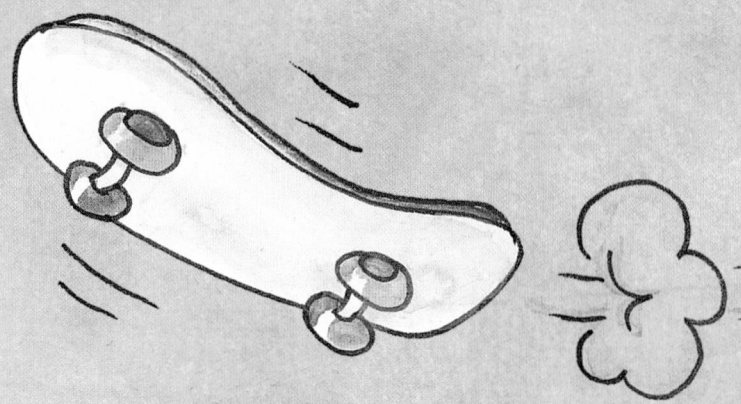

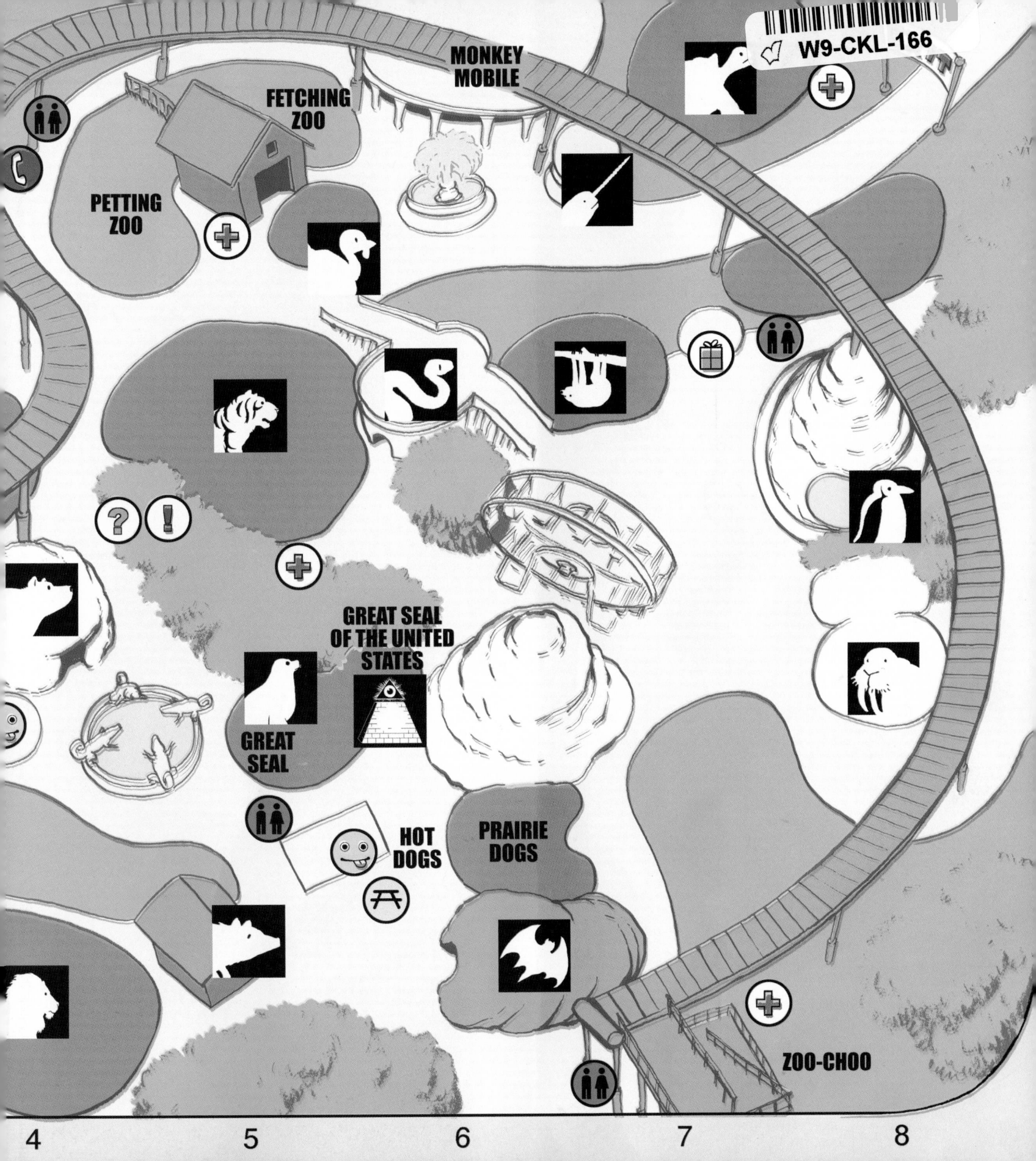

MONKEY MOBILE

FETCHING ZOO

PETTING ZOO

GREAT SEAL OF THE UNITED STATES

GREAT SEAL

HOT DOGS

PRAIRIE DOGS

ZOO-CHOO

4   5   6   7   8

HARCOURT, INC.

Orlando   Austin   New York   San Diego   Toronto   London

PRINTED IN SINGAPORE

I didn't know *where* I was
going to find all that stuff they wanted.

Luckily there was a
store across the street
that sold everything.

I wheeled back and gave the animals all the things they wanted.

I hope they enjoy them.

THE END.

www.HarcourtBooks.com

Library of Congress Cataloging-in-Publication Data
Rex, Adam.
Pssst!/by Adam Rex.
p. cm.
Summary: The animals at the zoo have some
unusual requests for a little girl who goes to visit.
[1. Zoo animals—Fiction. 2. Zoos—Fiction. 3. Humorous stories.]
I. Title.
PZ7.R32865Ps 2007
[E]—dc22   2006024551
ISBN 978-0-15-205817-3

First edition
A C E G H F D B

The illustrations in this book were done in oil and acrylic on watercolor paper.
The display type was created by Judythe Sieck and Adam Rex.
The text type was set in Clarendon.
Color separations by Colourscan Co. Pte. Ltd., Singapore
Printed and bound by Tien Wah Press, Singapore
Production supervision by Pascha Gerlinger
Designed by April Ward

This page has been intentionally left humor-free. The author actually knows
a very funny joke about Clarendon, but the punch line is a bit *italic*,
if you know what we mean.

For Tamson. She knows why.

—A. R.